Happiness is reading
your new book!

Phoebe Forrest Link

Small? Tall? Not at All!

author
Phoebe Link

artist
Chichi Walstad

Eifrig Publishing LLC
Lemont   Berlin

Originally published in 1973 by T.S. Denison & Company, Inc., Minneapolis (SBN 513-01297-4, Library of Congress Card Number 72-88721)

Published by Eifrig Publishing, LLC
PO Box 66, 701 Berry Street, Lemont, PA 16851, USA
Knobelsdorffstr. 44, 14059 Berlin, Germany.

For information regarding permission, write to:
Rights and Permissions Department,
Eifrig Publishing, LLC
PO Box 66, 701 Berry Street, Lemont, PA 16851, USA.
permissions@eifrigpublishing.com, +1-888-340-6543

Library of Congress Cataloging-in-Publication Data
Library of Congress Control Number: 2009938695

Link, Phoebe Forrest
Small? Tall? Not at All! /
by Phoebe Forrest Link, illustrated by Chichi Walstad

p. cm.
Paperback: ISBN 978-1-936172-02-3
Hard Cover: ISBN 978-1-936172-01-6

[1. Size – Fiction. 2. Imagination – Fiction. 3. Stories in rhyme]
I. Walstad, Chichi, ill. II. Title: Small? Tall? Not at All!

14 13 12 11 2010
5 4 3 2 1

Printed in December 2009 on FSC-certified 10% PCW recycled paper.∞

With joy, admiration, and abundant love
to my four grandsons:

David Robinson Link
Eric Forrest Link
William Harris Lehmann and
Matthew David Lehmann

Nana

Controlled Vocabulary List:

The words bearing an asterisk are on the Dolch Basic 220 Word List and are often known as "sight words." These words make up 75 percent of all the reading a child will do in the elementary grades.

*a	*could	*his	*me	ring	though
*all	dad	house	meet	rose	tippy
aloud	day	*how	more	sad	*to
*am	*do	I	might	Sally	*too
*and	even	*if	mighty	*say	toes
another	feel	I'll	moon	*see	tree
*as	feet	I'm	mother	shadow	*try
*at	flying	*in	mouse	shake	turtle
bad	*for	into	*must	shorter	twin
*be	friends	*is	*my	sister	*two
bear	*from	*it	neck	sky	*up
beat	gerbil	jam	*not	*small	*use
between	*get	Jonathan	*now	*so	*very
*big	giant	*just	*of	sometimes	walking
bigger	giraffe	king	*on	special	wall
bike	*grow	*knows	*or	stand	wanted
brothers	grew	land	others	tall	*well
*brown	*had	least	*our	taller	*what
*but	hair	*let	peach	than	*when
*by	Hall	*like	people	*that	*who
*can	hand	*little	pets	that's	wings
can't	*has	*long	*play	*the	*wish
care	helper	mad	Porter	*them	wishing
chair	he's	*make	proud	*then	*with
choose	hear	makes	*put	they'll	*would
climb	*her	man	reach	thing	*you
clothes	high	*may	really	things	young
cloud	highest	maybe	*right	*think	zoo
clue					zoom

To Parents and Teachers:

One of the most important tasks we as parents and educators have is to enable children to have a deep sense of worth and a healthy amount of self-respect. We need to help them affirm themselves for who THEY ARE.

As adults, most of us have some sort of limitation that we have learned to accept in life. This book is designed and written to encourage children to discover imaginative ways of solving problems in a creative manner. Most of us have forgotten what it is like to be too small to see over the edge of the table, to be the smallest one in the family (including the dog), or to have most of your friends in the neighborhood tower over you. But if we observe young children at play, we can gain a new awareness of this problem. For it is through play that they are expressing who they are and what they wish to be. Play is one of the most significant ways that children communicate to us their dreams, their frustrations, their hopes, their anxieties, and their knowledge of the world in which they live.

The vocabulary used in this book has been carefully chosen to provide a delightfully satisfying experience for the young reader.

Phoebe Link
January 2010

I'm small
I'm not tall
I'm small
That's all!

I play all day
And may
Hear people say . . .

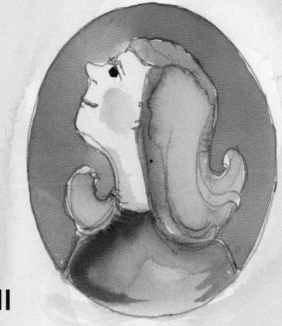

"He's small
He's not tall
He's small
That's all!"

7

I get sad,
Sometimes mad
And I wish I had

Friends
Who would say
All day . . .

8

"He's tall
 He's not so small
 He's tall
 That's all!"

9

What can I do? What would YOU do
if you wanted to be tall, not small?
If you wanted to be tall – that's all!

Well . . .

Maybe . . .

I could stand on
a chair . . .

Or on a bear!

11

Or with special care
Try to grow more hair!

I'll climb a tree
And then they'll see
I'm high and mighty
As can be.

13

If I rose
On my tippy toes,
Who knows
That it is me
 in long clothes?

I could wish for wings
Or flying things . . .

That would take me high
Into the sky.
(I might even zoom
Right up to the moon!)

A giraffe in the zoo
Is another clue.
I can climb his neck, too.

See how
I grew?

17

If I put my shadow on the wall
Then I'm really very tall.

Maybe a wishing ring
Would make me a king
Of tall, tall things
That I could use
Just as I choose.

But now
let me think
LET ME THINK
LET ME THINK!

Am I really so small
Not very tall?
Am I really small
Not tall at all?

Not really!
I'm in between.

I'm taller than my bike
And that's what I like,
I'm shorter than my dad
But that's not so bad.

I really can't reach
The highest peach

23

But when mother
makes jam,
Her BIG helper
I am.

24

Maybe I'm shorter
Than Sally Porter
But I'm just as tall
As Jonathan Hall.

I'm bigger than others
Like my little twin brothers
(Though my sister has me beat
By at least two feet).

I must be a giant
   to pets at our house,
The gerbil, the turtle,
   and the little brown mouse.

When I stand
    To shake the hand
        Of people I meet
            from another land . . .

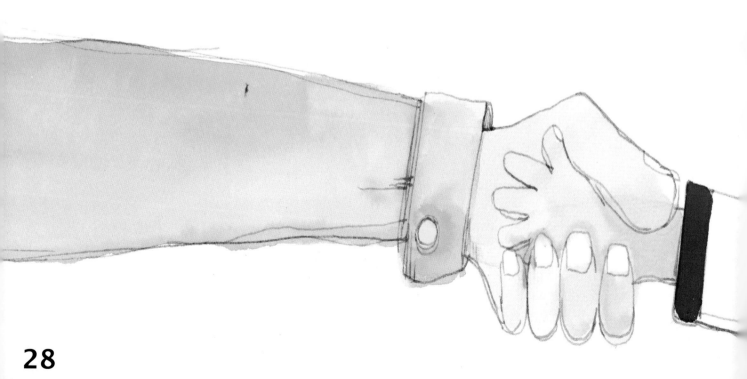

I feel so big and proud,
Like walking on a cloud,
When I hear them say aloud,

"How do you do,
young man!"

29

So. . .
When people say
All day,

"He's small.
He's not tall."

30

I say . . .

NOT AT ALL!